Knockin' on Wood
☆ Starring Peg Leg Bates ☆

BY LYNNE BARASCH

Lee & Low Books Inc. • New York

Photograph on last page copyright © Bettmann-Corbis

Manufactured in China

Book design by Tania Garcia
Book production by The Kids at Our House

The text is set in Fournier
The illustrations are rendered in ink and watercolor

10 9 8 7 6 5 4 3 2
First Edition

Library of Congress Cataloging-in-Publication Data
Barasch, Lynne.
    Knockin' on wood / by Lynne Barasch.— 1st ed.
        p. cm.
Summary: Presents a picture book biography of Clayton "Peg Leg" Bates, an
African American who lost his leg in a factory accident at the age of twelve and
went on to become a world-famous tap dancer.
    ISBN 1-58430-170-8
1. Bates, Peg Leg—Juvenile literature. 2. Tap dancers—United States—
Biography—Juvenile literature. 3. Dancers with disabilities—United States—
Biography—Juvenile literature. [1. Bates, Peg Leg. 2. Tap dancers. 3. People
with disabilities. 4. AfricanAmericans—Biography.] I. Title.
    GV1785.B3486B37 2004
    792.7'8—dc22   2003022905

To Don Emmons. His many students
will carry his good feet with them,
wherever they go — L.B.

Back in 1912 in South Carolina, when Clayton Bates was just five years old, he danced every chance he got. He had no shoes, so he danced barefoot. He had no music, so he made dance rhythms by clapping his hands and tapping his feet.

Clayton's mama was a sharecropper, raising cotton on a white man's land for less than she deserved. She had to accept the white landowner's payment whether it was fair or not. Her situation was common in those days in the rural south.

Clayton hated farming. To escape the fieldwork, he'd walk into town to the barbershop, where he could find an audience for his dancing.

At the barbershop Clayton danced for white folk, who threw him pennies and nickels. He did what was called buck dancing, not knowing it was really tap.

When Mama missed her son, she went after him and announced to the crowd, "You'll not make a monkey out of MY boy!" Then she dragged him back home.

That didn't stop Clayton. Nothing did. Dancing was what he loved best, and he did whatever it took to keep on doing it.

When Clayton was twelve years old, he asked his mama if he could go to work at the local cottonseed mill to get away from the fields. Mama didn't want him to do this. He was too young for factory work.

After many weeks of Clayton's pleading, Mama said, "I'll put it to the Lord and ask what to do."

The next morning Mama said yes, not sure if it was the Lord's will or if Clayton had simply worn her down.

On Clayton's third day working at the cottonseed mill, there was a terrible accident. His left leg got caught in a machine. The leg had to be amputated, but it wasn't done in a hospital. No such thing was possible for a poor black boy in the south in 1919. The operation was performed at home by local doctors, on the kitchen table.

No one thought Clayton would walk again.

Mama cried, "I must have heard the Lord wrong!"

Whether what Mama heard was right or wrong, Clayton's life would never be ordinary again. He had moments of deep despair, but there was something in his soul that wouldn't let him give in. He was young and full of life, and he had musical rhythms in his head that he just had to let out.

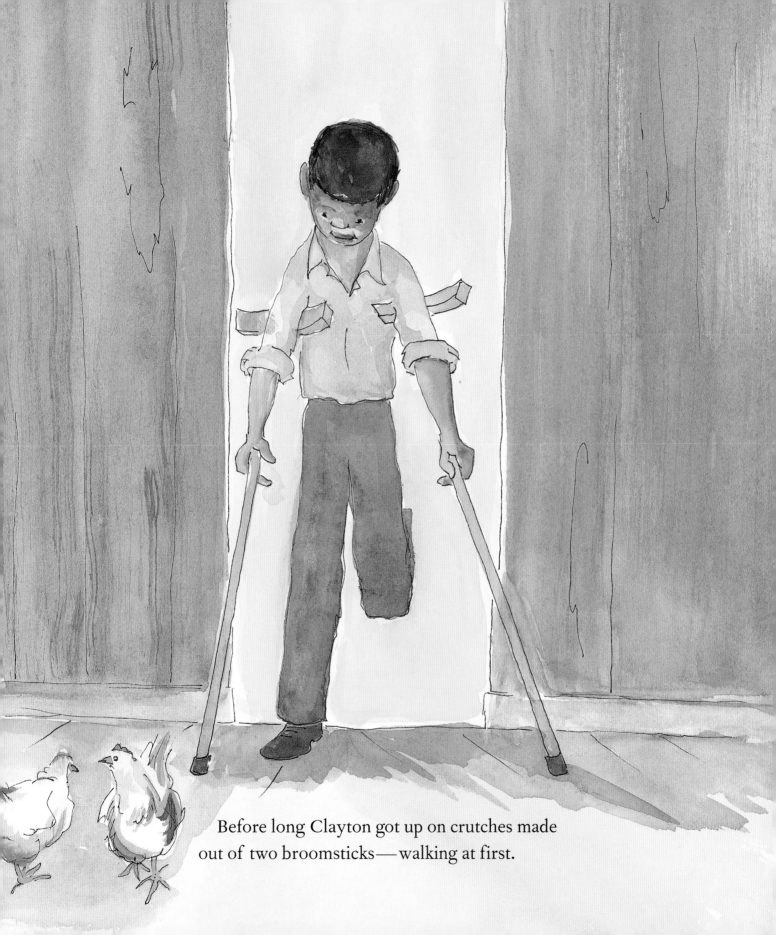

Before long Clayton got up on crutches made
out of two broomsticks—walking at first.

Soon Clayton was tapping out his rhythms with his crutches. He just had to dance. So his uncle whittled him a wooden leg — a peg leg. The tip was half rubber so he wouldn't slip and half leather to make sounds. On his right foot Clayton wore a tap shoe.

He created amazing rhythms all his own. Peg Leg Bates began to emerge.

As Mama looked on, she thought, *Dancing is his future, and there's nothing gonna stop him. Maybe it's for the best.*

He did all the usual Time Steps,

Cramp Roll turns,

Maxifords,

and Pullbacks.

But when Peg Leg did them, he created his own riffs.
Nobody had ever seen anything like his brand of rhythm tap.

Peg Leg began his career dancing for black audiences. He took pride in his appearance and wore a matching peg leg with every costume.

Peg Leg often finished performances with his own special dance step — the American Jet Plane. When he tapped across the stage, leaped five feet into the air, and landed on his peg leg with the other leg straight out, he always brought the house down.

He traveled the country with other black
performers, dancing in musical variety shows.

Peg Leg began attracting bigger and bigger audiences, and soon vaudeville theaters where only white performers and audiences were allowed wanted him on the bill. There, white dancers wore blackface. Peg Leg danced in this same makeup so no one would know he was black.

After the show Peg Leg wasn't allowed to eat near the theater with the other performers. Instead he had to go to restaurants in the black part of town to be served. Peg Leg endured this unfair treatment so he could keep on dancing.

Finally Peg Leg Bates gained so much recognition that there was no need for a disguise. He became a star performer, dancing at the Cotton Club in Harlem, New York, on the Ed Sullivan television show, and in movies.

He even danced for the
king and queen of England.

After appearing all over the world and often being denied
the opportunity to eat or sleep where he performed, Peg Leg
decided to build his own resort hotel where black people were
welcome. In 1951 he opened the Peg Leg Bates Country Club
in the Catskill Mountains of New York. For more than
thirty-five years, he performed there and greeted guests.

In spite of the adversity he faced, Peg Leg Bates never let
anything stop him.

"Black or white, one leg or two, it doesn't matter. Good is good."

"I was equal to or better than the best of the two-legged tappers. Nobody ever caught up with me. And there's been a lot that tried."

"Don't look at me in sympathy,
I'm glad that I'm this way.
I feel good, knockin' on wood.
As long as I can say,
I mix light fantastics up with hot gymnastics.
I'm Peg Leg Bates, one leg dancing man!"

Clayton "Peg Leg" Bates, 1907–1998